This LMER book belongs to:

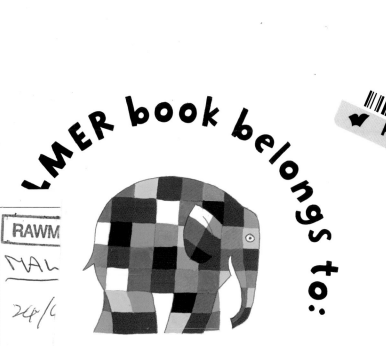

. . . .

This paperback edition published in 2011 by Andersen Press Ltd.
First published in Great Britain in 2011 by Andersen Press Ltd.,
20 Vauxhall Bridge Road, London SW1V 2SA.
Published in Australia by Random House Australia Pty.,
Level 3, 100 Pacific Highway, North Sydney, NSW 2060.
Text and Illustration copyright © David McKee, 2003.
The rights of David McKee to be identified as the author and illustrator
of this work have been asserted by him in accordance with
the Copyright, Designs and Patents Act, 1988.
Colour separated in Switzerland by Photolitho AG, Zürich.
Printed and bound in Singapore by Tien Wah Press.

10   9   8   7   6   5   4   3   2   1

British Library Cataloguing in Publication Data available.

ISBN 978 1 84270 981 8

This book has been printed on acid-free paper

ELMER
and the HIPPOS

David McKee

Andersen Press

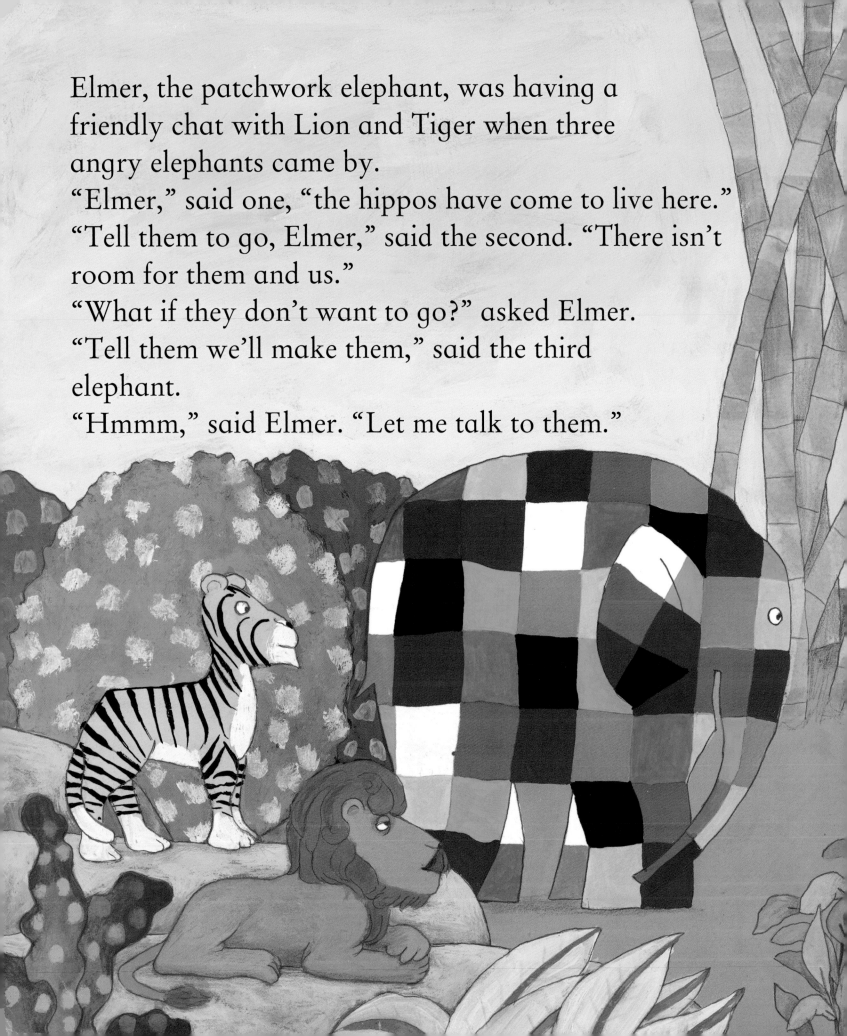

Elmer, the patchwork elephant, was having a friendly chat with Lion and Tiger when three angry elephants came by.

"Elmer," said one, "the hippos have come to live here."

"Tell them to go, Elmer," said the second. "There isn't room for them and us."

"What if they don't want to go?" asked Elmer.

"Tell them we'll make them," said the third elephant.

"Hmmm," said Elmer. "Let me talk to them."

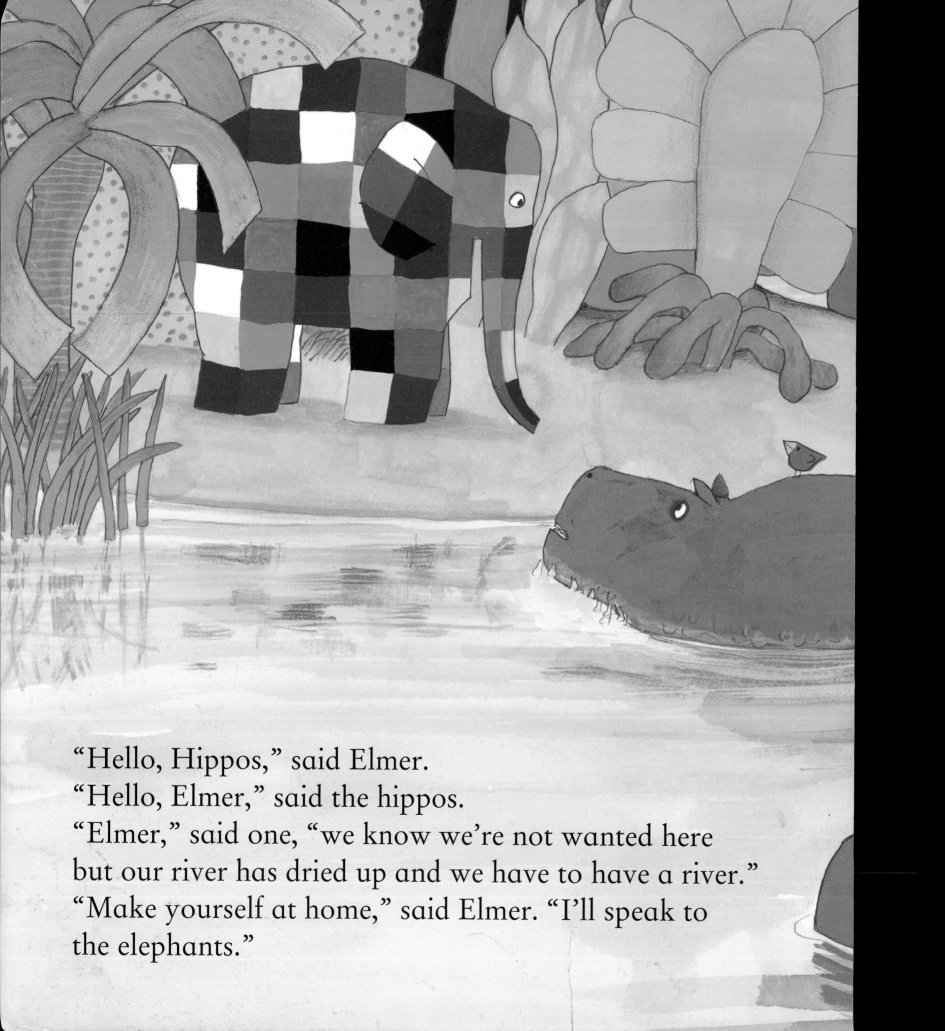

"Hello, Hippos," said Elmer.
"Hello, Elmer," said the hippos.
"Elmer," said one, "we know we're not wanted here
but our river has dried up and we have to have a river."
"Make yourself at home," said Elmer. "I'll speak to
the elephants."

Elmer told the elephants the hippos' problem.
"Imagine if our river dried up," he said.
The elephants agreed to let the hippos stay, but
grumbled because the river would be crowded.
"I'll take a look at their river," said Elmer.

The hippos' river was completely dry.
"Strange," thought Elmer. "I wonder what's happened?"
He set off along the dry river bed.

At last he came to some cliffs. The gap where the river normally flowed was blocked by a pile of rocks. "The rocks fell and stopped the river," a bird said. "Move the rocks and the river will flow again," thought Elmer. "But that means a lot of work."

On his way home, Elmer visited his cousin, Wilbur.
"Come on, Wilbur," he said. "I need your help."

"Good," said the elephants when they heard the news. "The hippos can move the rocks, get their river back and go home."

"It will take them ages," said Wilbur. "They don't have trunks. Still, they can stay here and use our river."

An elephant said, "If we help it will soon be done."

"Right," said Elmer. "Get a good night's sleep. We'll start early in the morning."

The next morning, Elmer called the hippos.
"Come on, we're going to get your river back. Are you feeling strong?"

The elephants and hippos were soon bragging about how strong they were as they marched along.

When they saw the rocks, the bragging stopped and they set to work, pushing and pulling them from the gap.

As the pile became smaller, they all became dustier. "I'd love a nice dip in the river now," said an elephant.

"Keep working and you'll soon be able to," laughed Elmer.

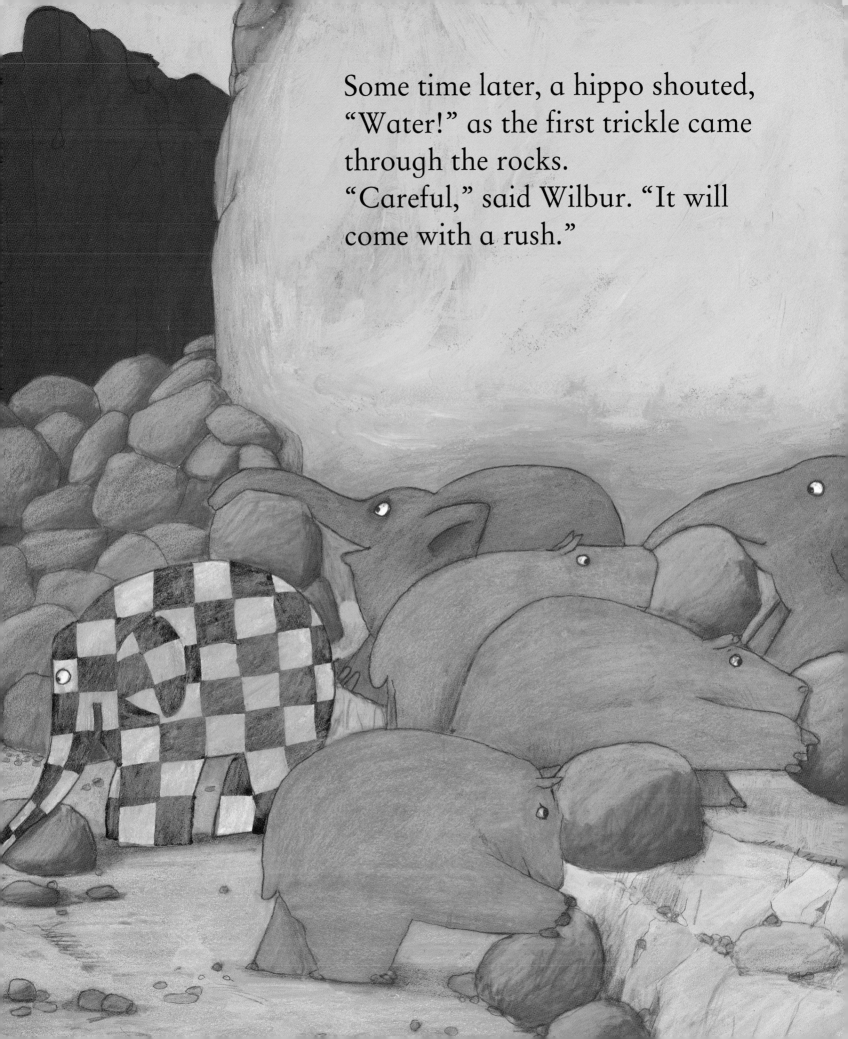

Some time later, a hippo shouted, "Water!" as the first trickle came through the rocks.
"Careful," said Wilbur. "It will come with a rush."

It did.
The water suddenly poured through, pushing the last of the
rocks out of the way.

Cheering and laughing, they all plunged into the river and forgot their tiredness as they washed off the dust and played in the water.

When they finally parted, the hippos thanked the elephants and said, "Come and visit us any time."
"You too," said the elephants. "Any time!"

Later, Elmer said, "You were all pretty friendly with the hippos in the end."
"Of course," said an elephant. "Besides, imagine if our river dried up?"

Read more ELMER stories

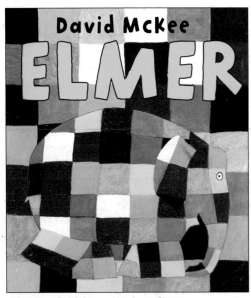

Also available as a book and CD

Also available as a book and CD

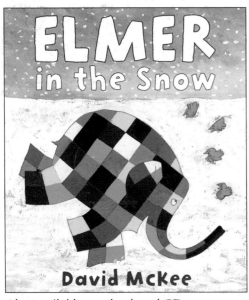

Also available as a book and CD

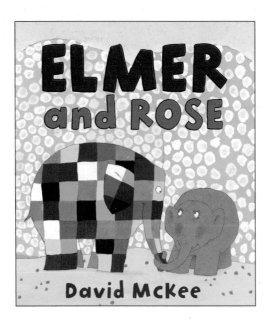

Also available as a book and CD

Find out more about David McKee and Elmer, visit:

www.andersenpress.co.uk/elmer